"I am too intelligent, too demanding,
and too resourceful for anyone to be able
to take charge of me entirely.
No one knows me or loves me completely.
I have only myself."

— Simone de Beauvoir

Also by Christopher Vinck

Poems in Celebration of the *Muse* *(Silver Bow)*
Ashes *(HarperCollins)*
Mr. Nicholas *(Paraclete Press)*
Augusta and Trab *(Macmillan)*
Songs of Innocence and Experience *(Viking)*
Only the Heart Knows How to Find Them *(Viking)*
Things that Matter Most *(Paraclete Press)*
The Center Will Hold *(Loyola Press)*
Moments of Grace *(Paulist Press)*
Finding Heaven *(Loyola Press)*
Compelled to Write to You *(The Upper Room)*
Nouwen Then: Personal Reflections of Henri Nouwen
(HarperCollins-Zondervan)
Love's Harvest *(Crossroad Books)*
The Book of Moonlight *(HarperCollins-Zondervan)*
Threads of Paradise. New York *(HarperCollins-Zondervan)*
Simple Wonders *(HarperCollins-Zondervan)*
Threads of Paradise *(HarperCollins-Zondervan)*
The Power of the Powerless *(Hodder) (Doubleday)*
(HarperCollins) (Crossroad Books)}

The Voice
Of
A Confident Woman

by

Christopher de Vinck

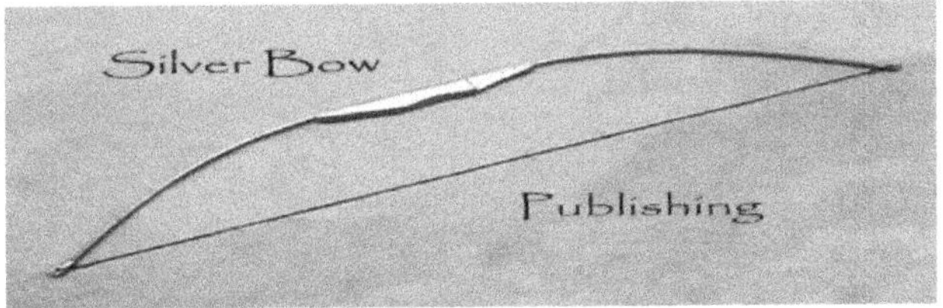

720 – 6th Street, Box # 5
New Westminster, BC
V3C 3C5   CANADA

Title: The Voice of a Confident Woman
Author: Christopher de Vinck
Cover Art: *Untitled*, ca. 1900, Emile Auguste Carolus Duran,
Layout/Design: Candice James
ISBN: 978177403 333-3 (print)
ISBN: 978177403 334-0 (ebb)
© 2024 Silver Bow Publishing

Library and Archives Canada Cataloguing in Publication

Title: The voice of a confident woman / by Christopher de Vinck.
Names: De Vinck, Christopher, 1951- author.
Identifiers: Canadiana (print) 20240520912 | Canadiana (ebook) 20240522273 | ISBN 9781774033333
   (softcover) | ISBN 9781774033340 (Kindle)
Subjects: LCGFT: Poetry.
Classification: LCC PS3554.E1165 V65 2024 | DDC 811/.54—dc23

To all confident women

CONTENTS

PART THREE
We are poised to speak each other's language

PART FOUR
You dance inside me.

PART FIVE
Do not love me if you do not love me sexually

CONCLUSION
I have made my choice after all

Author's Profile / 120

TWO TYPES OF WOMEN

She dreams a little, and she feels the dark.
—Wallace Stevens

There are women who prefer
A nightgown to sleeping in the nude,
Where cloth is better than loneliness
Against their skin.

There are women who ignore
A lost feather on the ground
Instead of placing it in their hair,
And extending their arms.

There are women who inhale
The aroma of the pungent orange,
And those who eat the flesh.

There are women who would rather
Swim in silence, and those who
Hear the ocean waves
Lapping against their breasts.

There are women who mock the moon,
And those who let the light of passion
Spin around their bodies like the rings of Saturn.

There are women who find comfort in prayer,
And those who moan in whispers
Under the hymns of those they love.

There are women who rise in the night
Beyond the horizon of their lovers,
And those who curl at the edge of their beds
And part their legs in obligation.

There are woman who do not guess
The fate of the seasons,
And those who mourn autumn graying,
And winter's cold, and spring's

Moment of beauty, and summer's songs.

There are women content
With curtains and tea, and those
Content with a man at their breast.

There are women who conceal themselves
In the folds of their cotton nightgowns,
And women who unfold the moon on their lips
And close their bodies around the bodies of the dream.

What sort of woman do you choose to be?

PART ONE

There is fire in my breasts.

A WOMAN'S INVITATION

Open the envelope of me.
—Anonymous

There is fire in my breasts,
Sparks made from embers
To burn your tongue.

Drink your desire
From my brown nipples.
Drain me.

I am greedy
For your mouth.
I want to possess
Your tongue.

I am more
Than a well to
Quench your thirst.

UNDRESS ME

There are two ways to reach me: by way of kisses or by way of imagination. But there is a hierarchy: the kisses alone don't work.
—Anaïs Nin

Wear the garment of my body
With all its folds and creases.

I am made of silk and your wishes.
Unbutton my breasts one nipple at a time.

Float the sleeves of my arms
Onto your arms.

Unfurl the hem of my thighs
And feel my fur is not fox or mink.

Sew me with the needle of your body.
Stitch your soul to mine.

A FEMINIST WARNS HER LOVER

She is so naked and singular. She is the sum of yourself and your dream. Climb her like a monument, step after step. She is solid.
---Anne Sexton

I write to celebrate your humid tongue,
And the key of your hands finding the
Treasures in my box.

I flare my breasts upward to your lips.
I am not made crudely.

When I am with you,
Silence moves beyond my hearing,
A distant moan, a spasm of air.

I will not die inside while you
Rummage through my body.
I will not turn my face away
And give you the impression
I am eager to turn into stone.

At times I try to find
The escape from your hands.
I look for an opening
Between your fingers
And find none.

What purpose love?
To massage the clouds
Hoping for rain?
To brave your collusion
With my thighs?

There are more surprises
In your ridged totem
Than in your wilting garden phlox

Touch the sand

Inside the hourglass of my body.
Watch each grain of time
Sprinkle on my breasts.

My body is not made of tin
But of ferns and dunes
And the surface of petals.

Do not enter me as if I am an animal.
I bleed poetry not blood.
I kick with my legs.
I do not have hooves as my feet.

Why do you pace inside me
As if you are a detective
Trying to solve the murder of my desire.

The streetlight of your phallus
Changes the color of my body.

If you place a blackberry
In your mouth,
You will know what I am
To your tongue.

I want to be horizontal.
I am not like your standing root.
I was meant to be approached like
Dawn, the dew of your body
Waking me with your summer lips.

I am exact.
Do not be clumsy
With your prodding.

I am the fire in the rose.
Burn between my petals.

Even nude stars shut themselves
Out and no longer blush at dawn.
Proceed cautiously along the
Cracks of my body.

I do not want to break
Into silent pieces.

A WOMAN'S THAW

One is not born, but rather becomes a woman.
—Simone de Beauvoir

I do not reside in winter.
My body is not cold and bare.
I am more the ornaments of spring:
The buds of my breasts in bloom,
The fresh stream between my legs
Open for the salmon
Of your body once again
To spawn inside my April thaw.

When love arrives in sudden heat,
I live inside my house this spring
With open windows. My soul is complete.

I am the vine of the clematis
Tangled round your post
With my blue tongue and
My blue breasts.

I am any flower you choose.
The ice that surrounds my body
Melts into the soil of you.

I was winter once. I wish to be
Your April spring.

Inhale my odor. Open my petals.
Touch my nectar. Pick me tenderly.

Enter the vase of my body.
I choose to be a woman.

A WOMAN'S REQUEST

To urge you to disgraceful acts.
—Joyce Mansour

I want to see you undress in the semi darkness.
Take off your clothes. Men are better nude
And you, my love, my desire.

You might think I am bold in my request.
The moon is more eager to see you strip.

I'd like to see how your roots and stems
Mingle with the shadows of my lust.

Open your shirt. Step out of your pants.
I want to watch you bulge spontaneously.

If you think a woman does not enjoy a nude man,
Watch how I toss your clothes behind me.

A WOMAN'S DESIRE

***I do not think there is a woman in whom the roots of passion
shoot deeper than in me.***
—Edna St. Vincent Millay

I am a woman
Who wants to bite your shoulder.
Passion is hunger.
Love is not a choice.
I can disrobe, but that is not enough.
I can tell you about magnolia blossoms,
But that does not explain the aroma
Of crushed petals between my palms.

No one knows that
When I bounce my hand
On the top of well trimmed hedges
It is your body I am caressing.

When I step out of the building
At the end of the day and inhale
The natural light and the tuxedo air,
It is you I invite to dance.

I am not a savage. I am not
A crazed woman
Who cannot control my hunger.
I just want to lower your shirt
And bite your shoulder
Because I love you this much.

A FEMINIST

O then, dear saint, let lips do what hands do:
They pray: grant thou, lest faith turn to despair.
—William Shakespeare

Let lips do what hands do:
Bloom together, feeling the pulse of the
Strong grip, the elastic touch,
The length of fingers, the tips of tongues.

I want to feel your hands
Weaving my breasts between your fingers.
My body is made of muscles and flesh.
I am not quartz or cotton.

Let me take your hand in my hand
And guide you over the continents
Of my body, the wilderness
Between my thighs, the Nile of my arms.

Passion is not a drum, or a collection of shells.
Passion swells in the heat of our Sahara.

Wear me like a necklace of stars,
The constellation of my body
Dressing you with my delirium.

I AM A LEOPARD

A man who dominates is a man who does not love. He has a tremendous animal vitality, a force, which conquers. He conquers, people are subjected by him, but he neither loves nor understands.
—Anaïs Nin

I want you to look at me as if I cease to exist.
Erase the lines of my waist.
Forget the snakes and fire in my hair.
Do not speak about the porcelain cups of my breasts.
You have looked at me long enough
As if I was a mannequin with moveable parts
To dress with your eyes according to the latest
Fashions: semi-nude, covered in silk or leather.
With buttons or no seams.

It is better that you stop comparing me
To your books: women in love,
Women on a beach, women on the verge
Of changing their legs into mermaid tails.

You do not understand the slick oil of a woman
Or the fibers of wheat in their loins.

Do you know women have hair on their legs
And under their arms and are savage
In their desires for the taste of oranges?
They like to peel the skin with their teeth,
Suck the flesh vigorously,
Roll the juice under their tongues.

I do not expect a miracle.
Men do not break from their stroking habits.
They do not know how to compare
A wax candle to their own monuments.
Men do not understand
The wick's labor inside the flame,
They do not understand the heat at the tip.

Leopards roll in dust for pleasure.

There are secret folds inside the flower.
Paris is a woman, jazz in my eyes.
Vanish in my womb. I leave scars of kisses.

I am my own need. I am a chamber of words
That echo confidence in my body.
I am your greenhouse in winter,
Always moist and warm,
The humidity of my body
Keeping your soil damp and loose.

I walk each day in the fire of my womanhood.
Each day I step out alive.
Touch me if you wish
To ignite me and not extinguish me.

A WOMAN'S QUESTION

In the swollen afternoon watch me undress.
—Anonymous

Why do you want,
To undress me before I undress.
Do you think you will find
Pearls on my chest,
Or hidden ferns between my legs?
Perhaps you are looking for
The slant of my waist,
Or you want to see
If my skin is equally right.
Did you want to see
If your hands will fit
Inside my hidden folds,
Or if your tongue will taste
What you imagine?
If you close your eyes
And kiss me once,
You will have all the
Knowledge you need of
My true nudity.

A WOMAN IN LOVE

The smooth folds of her dress concealed a tumultuous heart, and her modest lips told nothing of her torment. She was in love.
—Gustave Flaubert,

When love is in my care,
I caress lilies, and
Embrace the sleeves of my sweater
Against my chest.
I use the air to breathe your name.

When love is in my care
I define the wind as a thousand
Tongues on my breasts.
I am not an odd woman
With vines sprouting from my lips.
Your seeds do not
Crack open without moisture.

I am the theme of your desire.
I choose to be your song
From the throats of birds
And the sound of water in any stream.
Your hands cannot keep me still.
Your thoughts turn my skin into butter.
I become the moon, a pearl
Rolling on the body of your night.

My body is never slack
When I am with you.
I am not made of stone
When I am with you.
I am not a random joy.
I am the soil at the tip of your root.
The stars have less edges
When you touch me.

A WOMAN AND HER NEW LOVER AT MIDNIGHT

The swoon in the dark is lambs' wool.
—Anonymous

I am half night and half day.
Join me at this intersection.
If you bring me your male self,
I will bring you my female self.
You will have to rearrange my body,
Push my breasts aide for a moment
And look into my eyes,
And see my nipples in your eyes.

Please take my body and pretend I am not
A fish or a moon or any other thing
That you may want to enter
With your hook inside my open gills.

Be prepared to feel the difference
Between my body and your body
When we are joined at the hip
And surrender ourselves to salt and coral
As we rest on the wet sand of the shore
Where we are covered with our sea foam
As we blend into a spiral together
And swirl into a single shell.

A WOMAN ABANDONED

**Woman must come of age by herself...
She must find her true center alone.
—Anne Morrow Lindbergh**

You no longer listen to the sand of my body
Washing against the beach of your body.

You no longer taste the salt from my lips.
You no longer wash the pearls of my nipples
With your tongue while lolling on a towel beside me.

The corral necklace of my arms
No longer impresses you.
You no longer wear me as a jewel.

Why have you abandoned my words?
They no longer bathe with your words
Among the incoming tides.

What you hear is a white gull
Mourning the empty shell of a sea crab:
The flesh eaten, the shell filled with grit.
I am washed up from a tomb of sand;
My skeleton exposed, my claws open.

A WOMAN ALONE AT NIGHT

Quite alone. No voice, no touch, no hand....
How long must I lie here? For ever? —
—Jean Rhys

My poverty is draped
On the back of the chair at night
Like a robe of skin,
A body placed among the darkness,
And there in the bed a second reason
For sleep rising from the death of sleep.
I am no longer breasts or legs or bones even,
But an aura, a light or mist
That stirs with a voice,
My voice that asks for water
Or for a caress with your polished hands
That once mimicked the potter with his wet clay.

If you place your lips on my lips
You will not feel any moisture,
You will not find my will to open
To your touch for there is no more
Flowers in my body, no more seeds even,
No drops of honey for you to taste.
I am no longer made of earth and roots.
I am spent air, stale fumes rising from my chest
Above my bed, seeking an open window
As I float, not like a specter,
But more like a white flame seeking a shape,
Seeking a way back into the body of the mind,
Crawling back into the skin that I remember
Pulling the seams around my breasts and shoulders,
Admiring the fit, waking at dawn
With my blanket, like a shroud,
Painting the length of my body
Between my waking and dying.

You did not touch me once again.

A WOMAN ASKS

How bold one gets when one is sure of being loved.
—Sigmund Freud

Where can we be truly revealed?
Where do we become visible?
When light blots the darkness from our sins?

When clothes melt from our bodies
And we are ashamed?
Or does our truth step out of the mirror,
Mimic our voices, share secrets,
And claim we exist.

If a lover looks at our hands,
Does he see the coming pleasure?
If a lover touches our breasts,
Does it mean we are made for milk?

If we write about the seasons of our passions:
Spring lips, summer arms,
Autumn legs, winter shoulders,
Perhaps we are reveled in the full year.

Do not fear the shadows.
Challenge the light
To expose the truth of us:
The infinity of our existence.

THE RISING MOON

The moon is always female.
—Margre Piercy

A woman created the moon inside her.
Not a virgin birth. Saturn, Jupiter, even the sun
Took their turn to circle the moon with clouds
And the branches of trees and even
With the strings of a French guitar.

I thought it was at first the ocean
Lapping at her feet, pulling
Water towards her body, spilling
Shells and pearls deep inside her cavern.

She was in comfort, resting on the pillow
Of a velvet night, fertile with moon dust
And with silence at the rim of her body.

The moon provokes me with her breasts,
Suggesting milk, invites anyone
To inspect her wound.

She did not wait for the exact orbit.
She was not passive.
She felt the gravity of my touch.

I could have been idle, walking
Along the surface, measuring cures,
Calculating the waning and waxing
Of her skin.

Instead, I brought her roses,
Bleeding petals to show her
How flowers bleed with an aroma.

It was my intention to use
Her lips as a cushion,
To settle my lips on their silk.
I searched for her nipples

In the orchard leaning on the horizon
Of her body above me.

I was a traveler with a tent on my back,
Water in my leather gourd,
A telescope with polished glass.

I knew where to find her: among
The courting stars, among the bees swarming
Around her nectar.

I waited for the dance to subside,
For the sun to fully disappear into the night,
For the void to whisper her name.

I was not the acid wind stripping her body,
As she exposed her wound seeking
My healing salve.

PART TWO

Do not touch me with something soft.

A FEMINIST SPEAKS HER PREFERENCE

I want to sleep with you elbow to elbow
Hair entwined
Genitals enlaced
With your mouth as a pillow.
—Joyce Mansour

Do not touch me with something soft.
I cannot feel soft.
I know the feel of lamb's wool
And the lanolin between my fingers,
But that is not what I seek.
I do not want the tender side of the moon,
Or the half moon of your body against me.

You tried pouring sea water over my breasts.
I do not want water or salt
Unless it is from your tongue,
But even that is too delicate.
I want something hard and aggressive,
An ocean liner arriving at my port.
I want something hard, not cake
But a stick of licorice.

What I seek is not sweet but has the aroma of musk.
The Egyptians knew about the obelisk.
I will carve onto you my hieroglyphs with my tongue.
Look. I do not want a quilt with goose down.
I want the hardness of your body on my body
Lapping downward between my thighs like
The head of the salmon gulping into me,
Like the snake of Eden penetrating me.

I want the length of your hard love
Spilling into the soft love of my body
As equal partners in our desires.

A DREAM DOES NOT KISS

The beauty of darkness is how it lets you see.
—Adrienne Rich

Watch how a lover wears sunlight,
Loose like a kimono, buttons of stars
That you cannot see, a sash made of marigolds.

Use the sun for practice.
Seduce the heat with your body.
Speak to the beauty that caresses the globe
Especially at noon when she
Reaches her full power over
The terrain of your body.

Under her stiff gown of used moonlight,
A bronze softness bathes beside your hand.
She wears gold flakes of the Sahara.
Her lips are the color of honey,
Her breasts polished brass.

Secret happiness is hidden in
The saffron of her body,
A sweet floral flavor,
A taste of her soul.

As I wait for love I call out to the
Impatient stars and warn them
To stay in place and be who they are:
The bear, the twins, The bull of my body,
The scorpion of her tongue.
Sometimes I want to move the stars
And create beauty in the night,
The image among autumn leaves,
Or a horse, or beauty
From point to point
Connected with the lines of my imagination
As I read the new constellation.

I love her as any star,

Her breath of eternity that I inhale.

Beauty mocks the night
And builds a fire in her breasts.
I see the heat rising over the horizon,
Not star, not moon, but passion undressed,
The pulsar of her breasts,
Her thighs the open universe.

There is beauty in darkness
If we close our eyes.

Maybe heaven is the land of eternal seduction,
Love is the swan and the night air the lover.

I use small words to define her beauty,
And large words to sigh.
Passion is the language I speak tonight.

I know why I seek the moisture inside her breasts:
To swim, to drink, to
Find her soul in the liquid of her light.

She curls her arm into my arm,
Tangles my hair with her hands.
I linger under her touch.
A bear in winter knows the feeling of spring.

She expands like an egret rising,
Her choice to leave the cool water
As she opens her wings,
Pulls her legs upward,
And lets the turbulence of my body
Cradle her in the air of my arms
Until the new horizon, and once again
I dream no more.

A DREAM OF YOU AGAIN

***It had become a glimmering girl
With apple blossom in her hair
Who called me by my name and ran
And faded through the brightening air.
—William Butler Yeats***

Perhaps your breasts have the fragrance of teak,
Or the aroma of lichen and any stream
Or summer air that weaves against my lips
With your sudden care.

All parts of you tempt me:
The curls in your hair,
The driven land of your thighs,
The pennies of your nipples,
The planets of your eyes.

You are a festival:
The carousel of your arms
Around my waist,
The ride on the horse of your
Body rocking up and down
On the way to the
Gold ring of your passion.

There is a drowsy blaze in my sleep,
The coming of your warmth and kiss,
The dream that you shed your tail and fins
And turned from fish
To lips and tongue of your open bliss
With the ocean in your mouth
Where I drown and slip
Into a deeper, quieter night.
There is no better dream than this.

A DREAM SPEAKS TO A WOMAN

Deserve your dream.
—Octavio Paz

You deserve your dream.
Do not fear the slant of light
That caresses your breasts
Before you sleep.
It is not just the moonlight
From the window.
It is the day undressed,
The light made of moist air
Like a tongue on your nipples,
Like the whisper of a lover
Telling you he found your dream,
A broken flower in the garden,
And he wants to place it back
On the stem of your wishes
Near what you cannot touch.

You lie in bed among the thorns
That push up through the floor.
You feel the pricks on your lips.
You part your legs hoping
They are not thorns but kisses.
You do not believe in lips
Made of stones.

You remember what it was like
To have a hand change your body
From stone to water,
From darkness to the horizon
Of your body eager for
The open sun on your face.

Your body was not meant just for poetry.
Your body is more than hieroglyphs
In need of translation.

I read your body

As I read the skin of a dolphin,
As I memorize the sentences of your eyes.
I can be your dream with my books.
I can paint you with words,
Sculpt you with my hands,
Open the history of your body.
I can write the biography of your
Passion with a single word.

Point where you have been kissed.
Tell me the best place
Where you were injected with desire.
Can you mimic the sound you made
When you disappeared into the
Body of your lover?

You deserve your dream.
Life is the other, found
At the tips of your fingers.
Let passion mingle your body
With the comb
Of my teeth and tongue.

Mouths are not meant
Just for speaking.
Inhale the masculine air;
Smooth the space beside you
For my arrival.

Close your eyes.
You deserve your dream.

A KISS

A kiss that strayed
from your lips.
—Federico García Lorca

I caught
Your tongue
Like a
Circus act:
A seal
Leaping
Through the
Hoop
Of my
Mouth.

A ROOM OF MY OWN

***Yield to that strange passion which sends you madly whirling round the room.
—Virginia Woolf***

I live inside my body.
I arrange my room
So the light bathes
My dreams evenly.
If you want
To make yourself
Comfortable,
Sit here beside me
And tell me
About your room.

Is it filled with
The memory of books?
Do you still feel
The touch of a man
On your skin?
How many plants are
Growing in your room?
I hope you have an orchid.

You might think
My body is made of
Wood and plaster.
You might think
My walls are too empty and cold.
The heat is balanced.
There is a single door
With oiled hinges.

Come into my body.
There is enough room.

A WOMAN EXPLAINS HER SATISFACTION

My slender waist and thighs are exhausted
And weak from a night of cloud dancing.
—Huang E

We are exhausted after the night's cloud dancing,
To stay aloft in the mist of our love,
To encourage the moon to teach us lighter steps,
To swoon in the current of the night wind,
To feel the dew rising onto my breasts.

How close we were to heaven,
A blessing between our thighs
Where thunder was in his hips
And lightning in my eyes.

A WOMAN EXPLAINS HER WEARINESS

Tonight the Moon dreams with increased weariness.
—Charles Baudelaire

I admit I dwell in illusionary love:
Trinkets dangling on my body,
A necklace of your kisses,
The pearl of you tongue on my breast.

My body endures increased weariness
Stretched on the beach of your body
And I no longer feel
The rhythmic tides of your hands,
The curling foam of your hips.

I no longer care to taste your salt on my lips.

I remember how you lowered
Your satin chest onto my chest
And painted my eyes with your eyes
And how easily you fit inside the open wound
Of my body.

I am no longer cured.

A WOMAN EXPLAINS
HOW SHE IS TO BE SEDUCED

Each circle holds a secret.
—Anonymous

I draw this circle around me.
It could be a circle of fire,
Or my clothes stripped from my body.
I use my hand to point to the boundaries
As if my hand belongs to a hawk with shadows
Tracing my circle with his eager talons.

I surround myself with poetry
And with beads and berries,
With ancient relics from spring
From a time when we gathered
The teeth of bears to wear around our necks.

If you want to step into my circle
Learn how to dance,
Learn how to touch me
With the silk scarf of your tongue,
Wear bells on your ankles,
Recite a hymn to the stars.
I am a woman built with circles.
See the shape of my breasts?

If you would like to visit my center,
Lift the line of the circle,
Lift the hem of my dress,
And touch me with your circle,
And then we can spin until we
Are dizzy, and then we can die
For the evening until dawn.

A WOMAN INVITES A MAN
TO THE ART MUSEUM

I am a museum full of art.
—Rupi Kaur

Open the door to the main entrance.
I am not for windows and exists.
Enter the first gallery.
Look at each frame of me
As if I am Mary Cassatt.
Feel free to wander among the colors.
I can be abstract in this room,
And classical in the next.
I am made of Greek stone
And watercolors from Paris.

Do not speak.
The brush strokes on the canvas
Of my body speak to you.
Did you come for inspiration?
Do you look because your eyes are weary?
The guards will tell you not to touch
So close your eyes
And caress my paint with your fingers.
I am acrylic. I am dry with a rough surface.
Trace what you cannot see
With what you feel is hidden
Between the frame of my breasts.

When you enter the museum of me
Open you eyes.
Do not read the catalogues
For interpretations.
Step into me, mingle with my paint.
Fit inside the scene of me.
Let's be on display for eternity
Until the museum doors are shut again
For another harrowing night.

BY THE SEA

The sea, like a crinkled chart, spread to the horizon, and lapped the sharp outline of the coast, while the houses were white shells in a rounded grotto, pricked here and there by a great orange sun.
—Daphne du Maurie

Excavate my body with your hands.
Part the sand of my thighs and find
My curled shell cradled in layers.

Use the tides of your lips
To swim between my teeth and taste
The roots of my tongue
Made of sea grass and salt.

Unbutton my blouse.
Use my breasts as a chart,
My nipples stars in the
Constellation of Eros
Guiding you home.

THE LAMENT OF THE SEAMAN'S WIFE

Star kissing star through wave on wave unto Your body rocking!
—Hart Crane

Do you know a star can kiss a star
When the astronomers are not looking
And waves entwine like lovers
After the ships sink into the horizon?

You do not see what swells
Within my chest when you are away.

I partner with the stars and let them mimic your lips.
I ask the waves to unfold onto my body
And mimic the foam of your body
Licking my breasts.

When you are away
I voyage into your hands that I can still feel,
And trace the maps of your lips in my dreaming
So I remember how to find you
When you return to the wide port of our sea bed.

A WOMAN IS NOT A FANTASY

Love? Be it man. Be it woman.
It must be a wave you want to glide in on.
—Anne Sexton

Do not touch me without love.
I will disappear into colors you will never find.
You want to touch my breasts?
Do you know my name?
Do you know what I read?

Look at the curve of my spine.
Does it remind you of the moon?

Look at my eyes.
Are they the eyes of an invitation?
Do I look like a woman in need of your caress?

Of course I would enjoy the blanket
Pulled from my thighs.
Of course I would enjoy
You painting my body with your lips,

But if you are here for your own satisfaction,
If you will not remember my face,
If you exchange women's bodies
Like used milk bottles
You are speaking to the wrong woman.

Know who I am first
Before asking for the taste of my ordinary body.

A WOMAN LEARNING FRENCH

***I begin to long for some little language such as lovers use, broken words,
inarticulate words, like the shuffling of feet on pavement.***
—Virginia Woolf

I leave it up to you to interpret me
As if I am a foreign language
With strange sounding words for my breast,
With complicated passages as if studying Latin.
I am foreign to other lands.
India does not know the lavender of my skin.
I heard Japan thinks I am just a bamboo fan
Cooling the heat from your brow.

I am easy to understand.
Just listen to the murmur in my throat
When you caress the language of my body.
My breasts are French, my legs German,
The space between my thighs all of Asia.
Bring the ship of your body.

If you explore my continents,
You will learn of my traditions and customs.
The more you touch my breasts,
The more your lips form words on my lips.
You will begin to speak my language,
You will understand how one language
Borrows words from an another.

We will form a new language,
Write new poetry, create new prayers,
Live as if we are fluent nouns and verbs
With no punctuation.

A WOMAN PREPARES FOR HER LOVER

Eyes reveal the unsaid things. The innocence, the flirtations, and the naughtiness all emanate from the eyes.
—Avijeet Das

My love, I know the magic of bathing,
Unbuttoning my dress to the floor,
Stepping into the porcelain tub
Where the hot water applauds my arrival.

The water is the hand of your moisture
Cleansing me, striving for each crevice,
Splashing between the fur of my body,
Glazing my arms and shoulders
As if I am being immersed into honey.

I bathe to wash my soul and to feel the steam
Of my love for you rising.
When I step out of the water
It is as if I step off the shell-like Venus.

I dry my body with ferns and palm leaves.
I soften my skin with coconut oil,
So when you inhale me
You will think "How exotic."

PART THREE

We are poised to speak each other's language.

A WOMAN SPEAKS OPENLY ABOUT HER DESIRES.

...where we see with our tongues and taste with our fingers.
—Marge Piercy

We are poised to speak each other's language.
We no longer need an interpreter.
We learn the vocabulary of our bodies
And the function of each word in the sentences
Of our passions.

Passion is round, not triangular.
Let us sand the points of our bodies with our hands
And make ourselves into smooth circles
With the center of our primitive selves open to eternity,
Eternity until our final roar, gurgling desire in our mouths.

All the kisses we exchange are the tongues of panthers
Licking the submissive flesh of the antelope.

Do you feel the urge to paint my body with wet earth?
Do you yearn to become your hidden self naked?
Do you wish to expose your spear as I lay down my shield?
Listen to the sucking noise. It is not a draining stream
But the flow of your mouth
Tasting my breasts and the flavors between my thighs.

Undress me like an artifact hidden in the earth
Under the stones of your body.

I wish to be your clothes, to wear
The sleeves of your arms,
To unbutton the shirt of your chest,
To place your buttons in my mouth.

I long to pull off the belt that surrounds your waist
Like a snake; I long to swallow your venom of desire
From your mass of blood and extended flesh,
The cousin of the oak that grows down into the soil of my throat
Until your root nearly chokes me,

Until I can hardly breathe,
Until there is a panting and I long to gasp again.
You are buried like the bulb of a jonquil,
Nude, layered under my skin.
Are you prepared to extend your stem
With my moisture and heat?
Are you prepared to expand into a flower
For my lips to extract your nectar?

Couple me with the safety pin of your desire.
Unclip the sharp point. Penetrate me slowly

Then insert yourself back into the silver harbor.
With your needle, the severed folds of our bodies
Are repaired until dawn.

A WOMAN RECALLS LAST NIGHT

The hollow space is meant to be filled.
—Anonymous

I fell into sex, your body a pool of water.
I felt the depth and I did not struggle.
I knew how to swim, how to turn my head
And breathe and close my mouth in intervals,
And lift my face upward as I watched you
Dive backwards anticipating
Your silent splash and the spasm
Of disturbed essence for me to swallow.

A WOMAN RELENTS

I can give what you cannot have completely.
—Anonymous

I want to stand nude
Inside the ocean of your eyes.
I am that wide for your pleasure.

I want to sigh
Under the weight of your body
And feel your spring heat
Fertilize the earth of me
With seeds of lilacs.

If you sing my name from your lips,
And stand erect before me,
I will give you the right to love me.

A WOMAN REVEALS HERSELF

From behind the magic curtain.
—Anonymous

Love me with my shirt off.
Do not condemn my weak shoulders.
Revitalize my breasts with your tongue.
Remind me who I am beyond my clothes.
Call me a fantasy and I will be happy for you to
Unbutton my body for your pleasure.
I am still made of little secrets
Between the sugar cubes of my body,
A sweetness that melts under your tongue,
A reminder what it was like when we first
Discovered our bodies are more than
The movement on a hopscotch sidewalk
But more of the sidewalk for you to draw
Your numbers, a guide for your hands
Making sure you do not miss
Any place on my body.

Little tongues, little pleasure.
Large tongues, moist with history.
Divide me in the way you apply
The pressure from inside your mouth
And slather me with your intentions.

I am made for your pleasure.
Do not waste time with inhibitions.
Just undress me in a single movement
Like the magician does as he
Pulls the curtain to reveal the woman
Has returned from the disappearing box.

FLEX YOURSELF UPON ME

Love is composed of a single soul inhabiting two bodies.
—Aristotle

Flex yourself upon me,
Or inside me
With buttered love,
With salvia memories,
With semen soul.
I am not just a vessel,
A place for silt.
I am the full river
With the banks of my arms
Guiding your moisture
Out to the wide sea of ecstasy.

Keep me lonely if you choose,
But do not live inside
The dust and silence of regret.

I dare you to touch me.
I will not break.

A WOMAN SELLS

If there were dreams to sell, what would you buy?
—Thomas Lovell Beddoes

Dreams for sale! Dreams for sale!
What will you buy?
My breasts are discounted today,
Two for the price of one.
My lips have retained their value.
Here, feel the quality of my skin:
Silk not linen. It will cost extra.
My thighs are ripe
So there is no discount yet.
Shop at your leisure.
I have plenty of inventory.

t

A WOMAN SPEAKS ABOUT ETERNITY

I am lovely, O mortals, like a dream of stone.
—Charles Baudelaire

I am beauty, beyond mortals; I am not made of stone.
My breasts are offered as a taste beyond time
To inspire men to drink of acceptance they are not gods.

I can disguise myself as a sphinx on the desert sand,
Curl my legs under me as I kneel at the lip of the Nile
Suggesting my power to turn men into palm oil.

You can mix swans with the granite of my body,
Measure the softness in your hand and at the same time
Feel the cold slide of my skin if you touch without love.

Do not look at me as if you look in a mirror.
I am not a reflection of your desires.
I am eternity with an open womb.

A WOMAN SPEAKS TO HER LOVER
ABOUT THIRST

I will lie down lean With my thirst and my hunger.
—Edna St. Vincent Millay

What melts inside the mouth is not candy.
Ice perhaps? But ice does not satisfy the thirst.
What will stimulate the saliva? Beans? Meat?
I remember the taste of the orange,
And the way plums mingled with my tongue.

I drench my mouth with spring water,
And wet my lips.
I understand the sea is nude,
Exposing her pink shells on the beach.

If I could fit the liquid moon in my mouth,
I would swallow it slowly and keep the night
My private elixir.

Now that I have practiced,
I take the swell of you spilling into my mouth
And I am thirsty no more.

A WOMAN SPEAKS

I am as lovely as a dream in stone.
And, this, my heart where each finds death in turn,
Inspires the poet with a love as lone
As clay eternal and as taciturn.
—Charles Baudelaire

My breasts are not thorns to prick your chest,
But flowers, for your lips, filled with nectar.

My body is not made of fragments
But cloves, bits of moonlight, the fur of lions,
Secret fires that ignite the straw of your body.

When I open my robe
Watch how I am transformed
From what you thought you knew to
The new knowledge of my beauty.

I do not fade like the pictures of deer and bison
In the hidden caves of southern France.
I am your southern France.
I am the gazelle painted to your chest with
My tongue.

Do not burse your soul on my breasts.
Be a potter and shape the wet clay of my body
With your moist hands and your round kiss.
Spin me slowly and see my even proportions.

I am more than a clay dream, more than a substance
For your interpretation.
Do I need to convince you the curves of my breasts
Were stolen from the moon?

I am sweet to the taste if you know the taste of love,
If you extract the tender sugar cane of my body
And taste the juice.

If you are an astrologer I'd like you to lie

Under my constellation and touch each star.
Use your fingers to weave into my hair
Not a thousand serpents luring you
But more perfumed wheat for your harvest.

When you inhale beside me do you inhale my scent?
The aroma that lures winter into each spring flower.

Open your shirt, disrobe, let me spread my kisses
As snow geese on the copper lake of your body.

Let me migrate from the north of you to the south of you.

Join me in the waltz of our bodies.
Let me teach you the dance.
Let all your sorrows die on my breast.

Our love is not a dream in stone.
It is a dream we are painting.

A WOMAN'S CONFIDENCE

Woman: an adult female person.
—Merriam-Webster Dictionary

I am love. Flowers kiss me.
Bees penetrate my skin.
The moon is always nude.
Wheat bends to the harvest.
Shells mimic my breasts.
I invite the swan to embrace me.
I am lavender and basil.
I bathe in spices.
Incense is my lover.

SEVENTEEN POEMS IN TRANSLATION
FROM A 17th CENTURY GEISHA

I undress behind the silk screen of your anticipation.
—Anonymous

I

I am the woman under the plum tree in spring
Offering the fruit of my breasts
To the man with a ladder between his legs.

II

When I leave at dawn
Inhale the aroma on my pillow.
The bed will no longer moan.

III

When I walked out
To the field of bluebonnets,
I wished for the moon to seduce me,
But when you bathed me in your light,
I was cleansed of desire.

IV

The edge of my bamboo fan
Is not as sweet as your cooling lips
Waiting for my waving tongue.

V

The road to my body
Is between the sparrows signing
And you finding me nude
As I wait for you
In my room with the window open.

VI

You are a red winged blackbird
Clinging to the reed of my body
As I sway in the movement of your claws
Pleasing me.

VII

When I arrive I expect you to
Open the silk of my dress
And polish the fire
On my two dragons.
With your tongue.

VIII

I am the swan with open wings.
I will take flight if you
Are not the lake under me.

IX

The cock with feathers
Will wake you at dawn;
The other I use
To drink you to sleep.

X

The memory of your easy love
Drips like dew from the leaves
Of the sunflower.

XI

You said I am a rose.
I felt your thorn
Between my petals.
Perhaps you are the flower
And I am the vase of nectar.

XII

See the stones on the bottom
Of the jade pool?
Reach inside
And place them
Like my wet nipples
On the flat of your palms.

XIII

When I am alone

I use my arms as oars
And stroke the sea
Until I reach your mouth.

XIV

Time is nearly broken.
Hurry, the sun sets.
Stroke my breasts
So I remember
The eternity of you.

XV

If you whisper poems to me
When I sleep
I will you hear your words
In my dreams and
Part my lips and legs
And answer yes.

XVI

My body belongs
In a lighthouse,
My breasts pulsing
On the bow of your ship
Eager for you to safely enter the harbor.

XVII

Do you know why
My breasts have the aroma
Of magnolia,
Or gardenias?
I roll my body In the garden of your lips.

A WOMAN WHO TRUSTS AGAIN

Sometimes it is necessary
To reteach a thing its loveliness.
—Galway Kinnell

I need to reteach my breasts, again, to feel
What it feels in the hands and lips
Of a man who knows how to sign his love
On my body with his tongue.

You are the loving burn I remember
From younger men who lost their fire
When I extinguished them with love.

The wages of your body are coins to my eyes
Spilling, once again, like silver salmon
Between my legs.

I did not know I could live again
Until you touched my hair
And opened my dress with your eyes.

I told the moon I no longer believed
She held the sun in her breasts.

I kissed the mouths of many men
Who only knew the pressure of the tongue
And not the slow tenderness of my lips.

I no longer felt men entering me.
They passed through me
As trains pass through tunnels,
The engines of their bodies
Swooning in darkness
And I no longer knew their names.

I knew I could trust again.
When the scent of you roused me.

SAPPHO SPEAKS

In the crooks of your body, I find my religion.
—Sappho

You may think of me as a white rock,
Solid in my shape, curled in humility,
My arms and legs rolled around my head and chest,
A rag doll, a globe of flesh,
My spine curved like the edge of the moon.
But call me newly born in the womb of night.

You may watch me open my robe this morning
As the colors of resurrection wash over me:
Blues and greens emerging from my agony,
A distance from my strength.
I hope to share with you a part of what it means
To unfurl the pleasant joys of my body
Good for pulling and pushing to scorn loneliness,
But you must imagine I am the bold wind
Sweeping down the mountain around the single oak of you.
I am that wind, I am the one
To brave my flowing self around the trunk
Of the solid tree of who you are.

Recognize that I am in love with bits of the moon,
Engaged in the parting ferns as I walk towards you.
I am not a giver of pain but of healing.
My hands sew your wounds one caress at a time.
I toss aside the robe of my dreaming
And accept the hard earth of you under my body.
Acknowledge the soft bed of human passion
That is lulled but never satisfied.
I will not endure your fables and fantasies.
You will not find salvation
Between my breasts or in the prayers of my kiss.
You cannot embrace the sky with your arms
So why do you think I am that accessible?
Am I not just as vast, just as incompatible
With the small space of this room and bed?
I accommodate both the sun and moon

And every wide field prepared for the heat
Of the coming day.

Do not think of me as just a single flower
In the flat embroidery of your mind.
Are you a bee, a creature preparing to sting
At the slightest aggression?

Are you honey preparing to offer
The ooze of your sweet liquid at your convenience?

I am a white rock ready to transform myself
Into an ordinary woman, not a fool, not a convenience,
Not for the pleasure of the gods.

I lift the shade in my morning room
And welcome dawn with its warmth and light.

Mimic the sun.
Only then will I be your religion.

A WOMAN'S COURAGE

I am not made for despair.
—Ian Hearn

Standing nude before the lake
I am a woman able to mimic the blue heron
As she stands in the shallow water
Waiting to stalk her meal,
Or to open her wings and lift herself
In a sudden movement
To become a Japanese fan.

I, too, am waiting to step into the water
And transform myself into a heron,
A creature with feathers and a beak
Hoping to feel the water on my breasts
That remind me I am
Still able to seduce the water
With my body and sail upward
Like a blue heroin in ecstasy.

A WOMAN'S LOVE MAKING

I only believe in fire. Life. Fire.
Being myself, on fire, I set others on fire.
Never death. Fire and life.
—Anaïs Nin

The sea has no fear, for the sea has depth.
The chasm for tourists opens wide
For anyone to explore
And see the layers of crushed earth,
Centuries past, the brave earth
Open, the river that cuts
Into the gorge, making the earth give way
At its weakest point.

No life survives on granite.
Dense desires have no place in shallow living.
Let the earth and water spin in unison,
Not in chaos but in mutual labor
To create a fertile ground for our love making.

I need your arms and legs
To hold me still as the stars attempt to
Drag me into a molten sky of ether
Where I cannot feel the orbit of you pulled
Into the heat of my gravity.

Restrain me with electric kisses
And with your imagination
And I will know the difference between
The flesh of your lips and the hot silver kiss,
The richness that dissolves into the combined
Taste felt, when ignited.

It is not the hot sun or moon combined,
Not the cold air against the heat of our bodies,
But love and soil, the sap from our hollow places,
That merges to form ourselves joined
In, this, our burning hours.
Take my cold shadow and kiss my cold shadow

And you will find no color, no stable shape,
But tease the flame of my shadow
With the shape of your body,
Watch how my arms stretch, and my legs open
With the sun behind me and you will
Know the gray outline of my face and breasts
And the softness in full curves and rest
Against not shadows and the taste but with
Hot oils and sex, my perfume sprayed
On your open palms for my caress.

Do not barter for parts of me.
I am not made of stones or bits of lavender.
I am many women: a bird, a serpent,
A slab of marble, a beach of soothing sand.

I am all at once a fire and will burn you
At your touch, and swallow you with
My lasting flames that slather you with
The embers of my passion as I
Watch you writhe and live in my
Star-heat desire.

PART FOUR

You dance inside me

YOU DANCE INSIDE ME

You dance inside my chest, where no one sees you, but sometimes I do, and that sight becomes this art.
—Rumi

You dance inside me. You walk inside me.
You are silent inside me. You rest inside me.
I feel the movement
Of your feathers inside me.
You are a swan, a sparrow,
Perhaps even Poetry with wings.
There is no telling
How much space
I have reserved for you
Among all the rattle and
Movement between my ribs.
Even when you have no time,
Linger inside me.
Touch what you want.
I am not made
Of brittle antiques.
When you are finished
With my interior
Bring your hands dipped in oil.
Feel the silt of my skin.
Measure my breasts
With your tongue.
See how your body
Fits on my body.
Dance beside me.
Walk beside me.
Rest beside me.
Drape the feathers
Of your arms around me.
When the inside matches
What is outside
Then you will have found
Love and passion combined.

A WOMAN'S PREFERENCE

A flower blossoms for its own joy.
—Oscar Wilde

Do flowers keep secrets from one another?
Do they share how they became blue or red?
They breathe air and sunlight slathers on their petals.
Flowers listen for the coming rain
To nourish their roots.

Inhale the aroma between the breasts of a flower;
The bulbous shape will express an allure.
Flowers are not modest, not sisters but lovers.
Flowers hold seeds dipped in their sap,
Some secrete milk.

Flowers bathe in public, reach upward when it rains,
Expose their full shape glazed with water.
You might confuse the sex of flowers
If you just take notice of their rigid stems,
But all flowers are more feminine,
Made of pleats and nectar on their lips,
And pollen to caress their neighbors.
There are flowers that prefer loose soil,
And others hard clay.

A WOMAN'S WISDOM

There is no-one a wildish woman loves
better than a mate who can be her equal.
—Clarissa Pinkola Estés,

Do you stretch nude above me
For your pleasure,
Or for my pleasure?

Do you suck my breasts
To stimulate your body,
Or to simulate my body?

Do you watch how my eyes move
To see if I am attentive,
Or to see if you are attentive?

When you part my legs,
Are you making room for yourself,
Or are you making room for me?

When you lower yourself
Between my thighs,
Are you entering me,
Or am I entering you?

In love we cannot
Tell the difference.

A WOMAN'S BODY IS MADE OF MOONLIGHT

How sweet the moonlight sleeps upon this bank!
Here will we sit and let the sounds of music
Creep in our ears: soft stillness and the night
Becomes the touches of sweet harmony.
—William Shakespeare

In the blue light of the moon, the light
That filters from the summer night,
You walk nude without
The shape of breasts and legs,
And without the movement of your hair.

In the dark you have no dimensions.
There is an aura, similar to the Northern Lights,
A shimmer of light like the lake water
Swallowing the reflection of the writhing moon.
The regions of your body sway into colors:
Beige, tan, even the color of pearls
And magnolia blossoms.

In the blue light you become less stable.
I cannot see your face.
Your beauty becomes translucent.
I can see through you, and see the distant mist
That is your body floating in the moonlight.
You are not a mirage.

A WOMAN'S DESIRE AFTER THE FIRE

I want to sleep with you elbow to elbow hair entwined,
genitals enlaced with your mouth as a pillow.
—Joyce Mansour

I want you in the bed of my arms
Resting on the pillow of my breasts.
I want you to feel the horns of my body,
The tips that spill milk
When I enter your mouth.
I want you to breath me,
Inhale my body that does not lie.
My body tells the truth of my desires.

Peel off my clothes.
Taste my flesh.
Suck the juice of my body.
Do not spit out the seeds,
Swallow the seeds and let me
Fill what is empty inside you
With orchards of my passion.
I want you in my bed of eyes
So that I can look at your stillness
And hear your slow breathing
After the fire.

A WOMAN'S DOUBT

Truth isn't solid. It's liquid.
—Joshua V. Scher

I do not know if
I can keep spilling
My body over you.
Yes, I am liquid,
But Sea liquid, Lava liquid.
I flow from the earth,
And not from the moon.
The stars of
What you imagine
Do not melt my breasts.
I do not fit inside
Your cup to drink.

If I touch you
With my body,
Do you feel the moisture?
I am part rain and part dew.

Too much heat,
And I evaporate;
Too little passion
And I become stone.

A WOMAN'S ERROR

There is no shelter in you anywhere.
—Edna St. Vincent Millay

I am exposed in your arms.
My body is unclothed.

Your shadow does not keep me warm.
As you place your body over my body
I do not feel secured to the earth.

If I enter the cave of your mouth,
I cannot hear you speak.

If I come to you for comfort,
You prod me with spears.

There is no shelter in you anywhere.

A WOMAN'S EXPLANATION

I would blossom if I were a rose.
—Edna St. Vincent Millay

At your kiss I would blossom if I were a rose,
I would change from a chameleon's hue to your color.

At your touch I would become new gold
And your crown; the crown of Midas.

Under your hands I would writhe if I were a fish
And feel my gaping mouth swallowing your water.

When I am under you I may as well be sand
As you stir me into a dune.

A WOMAN'S INDEPENDENCE

*I am too intelligent, too demanding, and too resourceful for anyone
to be able to take charge of me entirely.
No one knows me or loves me completely.
I have only myself.*
—**Simone de Beauvoir**

I belong to no man.
I do not break.
I am not fragile as glass.
If you place a seed in my mouth,
I will spit out the garden of you.
I bathe in the water of my books.
I eat the fruit that dangles from my pen.
If I desire a caress,
I check for the turbulence in the air.
If I am hungry, I eat the memory of you
And wipe my lips with my independence.

A WOMAN'S LAMENT

Mine is the body that should die at sea!
—Edna St. Vincent Millay

If I could choose I'd live another way,
Spill water from the sea over my body
And become a fish,
Cover my body with blue scales,
Inhale the water through my gills,
Wear pearls and coral,
Abandon the shape of my breasts
And be more fish than woman.

I'd writhe on the beach sand
In the dying air
And hope you would come
And toss me back into the sea foam
Of your passion.
I am not built for nets
Or for a glass aquarium to be admired.

I am meant to bathe in the currents
Of your body,
Leap above the surface of your chest,
Expose my body to your sun.

I do not wish to be speared.
I do not wish to endure
A hook in my mouth.
I do not want to be mounted on a wall.

I wish I could belong
Inside your tumbling sea
And be your only lover.

A WOMAN'S LOVE POEMS
TRANSLATED FROM THE 17th CENTURY JAPANESE

My body is a silk fan for your pleasure.
—Anonymous

I

I give you my nipples to cure you of your thirst.
Drain me until you sleep.

II

The bamboo of your body is firmly rooted in my soil.

III

When I think of you I think your hand
is a tongue that moistens my body.

IV

The seasons are my breasts for the calendar of your body.
Count the days.

V

Stripping nude for you is like painting my shadow with my flesh.

VI

At dawn wake me with your lips between my thighs
and I will be your open horizon.

VII

Touch my breast and see how much I resemble the rose.

VIII

Know my dream of you blossoms into the shape of a mushroom bulging
upward from my moist earth.

IX

The shrill of the cicada mimics
the voice of my orgasm inside your summer heat.

X

Sleep with me tonight. I have a new silk pillow.

XI

When I inhale the incense
At the evening: my temple, your musk.

XII

I mimic the moon because I want you to see me nude.

XIII

I take you in the nest of my mouth
As if you are a bird with a hard beak.

XIV

The geese on the pond mimic my hands on your chest.

XV

I like how your hands dry my breasts after a bath.

XVI

Love me now. My fruit is ripe.

XVII

Drink between my thighs. I will hold your head
To steady your lips.

XVIII

When I am alone, I place my finger in my mouth and suck you.

XIX

My silk robe may as well be your body.

XX

Know that the pressed flower in my letter touched my lips.

XXI

See the fireflies touching the darkness?
My lips flashing on your chest.

XXII

Do not expect me to undress unless you know my name.

XXIII

My body cannot maneuver
The sea of my passion without your keel and rudder.

XXIV

Your mouth is the great heat.

A WOMAN'S MANIFESTO

What should I be but just what I am?
—Edna St. Vincent Millay

You will not possess me
As the moon posses the tides.
You will not dominate me
As the ether encircles the globe.
You will not restrain me
As the night binds the stars in place.
You will not own my body
As dawn has all rights to the horizon.
You will not govern me
As your own private country.

I am the moon
Possessed in my body.
I am the tides
In the flow of my blood.
I am the ether
That you breathe at night.

My arms and legs are
Shackled to my own desires.
I decide where to place
The stars of my kisses.

Dawn is my nudity
Exposed on the horizon.

I am my own country,
Population one.

A WOMAN'S NOTE TO HER LOVER

I found lingering evidence of your passion.
—Anonymous

Last night
The stain of your love
Seeped through the cloth
Of my skin,
Spread deep within
The material.

Your liquid substance,
A fluid expression
Churned up
With the purpose
Of leaving your body
To enter my body,
Was an exchange
Like moonlight blending
With sunlight at dawn
Illuminating the horizon
With a red and yellow
Glaze on the world.

You are the horizon's light
On my legs, on my arms,
On my breasts and hips.
I see the mark you left
Behind.

I have been baptized
With your body.

You are indelible.

A WOMAN'S PLAN

Fortune befriends the bold.
—Emily Dickinson

I will provoke you with my dress,
My shoulders exposed,
The downward slant of the cloth
With the hint of my breasts.

I want to watch your eyes widen
With my beauty I half disguise.

I want to hear a tremor in your voice
As you greet me at the airport.

I will seduce you in public on purpose.
I am that bold.

A WOMAN'S PREROGATIVE

***There is nothing revolutionary whatsoever about the control of women's bodies
by men. The woman's body is the terrain on which patriarchy is erected.
—Adrienne Rich***

What do you want to erect on my body,
A derrick to siphon the oils from your body?
If you are tangled in my body,
You cannot see your own thorns and petals.

Do not dream inside me
Unless you first dream within yourself
Before you slather me with your tongue.
If you believe my body is a monster,
Swallow your own sword
And slay yourself with sorrow.

My beauty is my own possession.
I only lend it to you for the evening.
You can only purchase my beauty
With the money of your heart
And with the value of your lips.

If you do not see my modesty
With my beauty,
You do not understand love.

Remember the earth in the beginning?
I am the earth in the garden. I am Eve.
You cannot colonize me. I am a revolution.
My clothes are obstacles to beauty.
Unclothed I am the taste of your desires.
I will not be your meal.

My nudity is a secret except for
Those I love, for then I give them
The code of my voice
And the combination for their hands
That unlocks my body.

PART FIVE

*Do not love me
if you do not love me sexually.*

A WOMAN'S SELF KNOWLEDGE

I am moist between the legs.
—Anaïs Nin

Do not love me
If you do not love me sexually.

I am fire and I need
The cool water of your hands.

There is no such thing
As moderate ecstasy.

Drink me as wine not as sand.
Unwrap me
With your hands and tongue
In our collusion.

I am near to madness.
I can almost touch it
With the tips of my breasts.

I want your hands
To be a calming sanity.

Do not be explicit,
Approach with slow suggestions:
The slight parting of your lips,
Curiosity In your fingertips.

I am a kiss and
Your imagination.

Sink your body into me,
The well point
Finding water.

I am moist
Between my legs.

A WOMAN'S SPRING

And spring arose on the garden fair,
Like the spirit of love felt everywhere;
And each flower and herb on earth's dark breast
Rose from the dreams of wintry rest.
—Percy Bysshe Shelly

I do not reside in winter.
My body is not cold and bare.
I am more the ornaments of spring,
The buds of my breasts in bloom,
The fresh stream between my legs
Open for the salmon
Of your body once again
To spawn inside my April thaw.

When love arrives in sudden heat
I live inside my house this spring
With open windows.

I am the vine of the clematis
My white breasts tangled round your post.
I can be any flower you choose.
The ice that surrounds my body
Melts into the soil.

I was winter once.
I wish to be
Your April spring.

Inhale my aroma,
Open my petals, drink my nectar,
Pick me tenderly.
Let me enter the vase of your body.
I choose to be a woman.

DESIRE

**If we go down into ourselves, we find we possess exactly what we desire.
—Simone Weil**

I would like
The circle
Of your face
Between
My breasts
As you
Use the tip
Of your
Tongue
To find
The sting
Of my
Nipples
That will
Pierce
The lips
Of your
Desire.

A WOMAN'S ULTIMATUM

No longer for your pleasure; no longer self for self.
—Anonymous

I am not made of sand
That shifts into dunes under you.
I am not a lily meant
To cover your legs with pollen.
If you think my breasts
Are to tickle your tongue,
If you think the space
Between my thighs is made for you
To probe with your body,
Tell me, when was the last time
You were used as wood to burn
Or felt an obelisk
Collapse on your face?

When was the last time
Your chest was polished to a dull surface?
Do you like being prodded
Between your legs with a piston?
Do you like the odor of skin?
Do you like to stare at the ceiling
While being used as a dry well?

Do not disturb me.
Watch how sparrows
Peck at seeds
In the glass feeder.
They are selective.

If you want my body
For the afternoon
Kiss my forehead
Like a blessing first.

A WOMAN'S WHISPER

I want the bridge of you.
—Anonymous

I want the bridge of you
Spanning the river of my thighs,
Your girders and cables
Supporting the arch of your body,
As the water of my body
Circles the foundation of your column
Embedded in my riverbed,
As the silt of my breasts and kisses
Settle beneath you.

A YOUNG WOMAN'S DATING FRUSTRATION

I am not a possession or a bauble.
—Anonymous

I am tired of looking at men with my magnifying glass,
Watching them increase to twice their size
As they, in their pleasure, extend their buds into blossoms
With the delight of new heat and water.

I no longer wish to be that heat
Or that water with my hands and body.

Why must I serve their pleasure
Before they find their way into my body?

Why are men so possessive of a single appendage
When I am a complete body,
A whole movement towards love?

Why do men feel when they are exposed?
They revel in the truth of who they are.
Men ought to be less internal and more
Exposed with their lips and eyes
And speak to me with petals and books
Rather than with their engorged skin
And bulbous tongues that speak when
Extended between my thighs.

ADVICE TO WOMEN IN LOVE

Go wisely and slowly.
Those who rush stumble and fall.
—William Shakespeare

A man will become liquid,
If you drink him.

A man will become a panther,
If your drape his skin
With your darkness.

A man will moan,
If your burn him with your lips.

A man will divide you, if you
Show him your borders.

A man will be hard,
If you are soft.

A man will whisper your name,
If he feels your signature
On his chest.

ADVICE TO THE COURTESAN

Inside the hidden chamber of the palace
—Anonymous

Wait for him to return to your bed,
Wait with your clothes shed
In the hour of the dream awakened.
Arrange what he likes:
Books of poetry, bluebonnets in a vase.
Perhaps prepare the phonograph
And preset the needle on the record to
Spill the moon river around his body.

What robe will you wear?
Will it be transparent?
Will it be the one with silk roses?
It is appropriate to leave your door open
As you call out his name
Suggesting there are hawks in the room
Eager to ravish his flesh with their
Beaks and talons.

ADVICE TO WOMEN:
DO NOT FALL IN LOVE WITH A WRITER

Men who write only image my breasts.
—Anonymous

When I dress in red I am nude just the same.
I have more value than a thousand statues
In the museum of Rodin.
Men touch marble not the truth
Of a woman's breasts.
Women give themselves once
And know the difference between
The taste of a man
And their appetites.

Men think they know the surface of my body
That is the least of my unfolding.
If you touch my waist
Prove you know how to dance.
If you want to enter my mouth
Explain what it was like to swim in the Sargasso Sea.
Memorize the contours of my face
Not the topography of my hips.
A woman is not a canvas to paint with stokes of desire
Of at the tip of your repressed power.

My name is Eros. My name is Sappho
My heritage is hidden in the flesh of Eve.
Listen for the faith echo of Venus in my throat.
Treat me as if I am sister to the moon,
Cousin to every flower: potent, unique, a contender.

A Woman's heart beats inside her body
Not inside a man's quill.

ANNE SEXTON AT HER DESK

As for me, I am a watercolor.
I wash off.
—Anne Sexton

Do I write about madness?
Do I call it daffodils and porpoises
Or the color in my eyes
Or the veins in my long legs?

Are you attracted to my folly,
The size of my breasts, my need
For attention, the center of body
To make the cherry poem,
Or the nude play of myself sprawled
On your couch for therapy?

Read me as if you are reading my body.
I am a constellation; my children my comfort.
I swim nude because I am the moon.
Have you ever seen the moon wear a bra?

Kiss my poems and I am your mistress.
Undress my poems and I will abandon you.
And I will hurt you with my silence.

Look, this is the desk where I write.
That is all you need to know,
Unless you want to love me.

ASSEMBLY NECESSARY

I am a woman. Assemble me.
—Anonymous

Come to my body.
There are no instructions.
I have no secret life
In the poetry of my breasts.
You will find your own
Rhymes and rhythms
At my kiss.

Unfold each part of me carefully.
I need to be assembled.

Each connection is essential
For a flexible fit.
If you come across
Wings or feathers
Ignore those extensions.
Focus on what you understand.

You will find I am not an empty dress
But the full form that fills your desires.
Read the guide of my body carefully.

Do not misplace any part
For they are all necessary.
If you use your hands
Be careful you do not
Snag your fingers in my hair.

Keep your tools oiled.
Open my buttons of light
One moon at a time.

Come. I am spread out before you.
You do not need to be a craftsman.

THE MOTHER SWIMS NUDE
WITH HER THREE GROWN DAUGHTERS

Mothers: teach your daughters how to be nude.
—Anonymous

I am the mother with a single lesson,
Oh my daughters who are now transformed
From straight lines to the curves of the moon.

You recognized my voice, helped me
Arrange the combs in my hair as children,
Gathered straw flowers in autumn for my pleasure.

I bring you now what I know to be secrets that hold
Deep within your bodies bright for new meaning,
An exposure, an acceptance defined as women.

Watch how I shed my clothes. Do not be embarrassed.
Look, I am made for love; the body is made for love.
I am made for milk at my breasts. The body nourishes.

See how the hair joins my hips in the center,
This place for new beginnings, a portal to eternity born
An eternity that does not die in the tautness you will feel?

See how I step into the water? We are made to be nude
In the water, made to feel the water mold to our bodies.
I close my eyes. I fan my arms in the water. We are the water.

To be in the lakeside edge is as close to flight we shall come,
Floating in lightness we cannot shun,
This place that accepts us in our bold revelations.

Come my daughters. Now it is your turn.
I have shown you how.

A WOMAN TO HER LOVER

The center of a woman is not just between her legs.
—Anonymous

If you see the center, focus on the center.eware, the center exposed
burns with heat,
The heat stirs the roots in spring,
Churns the ocean currents, and warms the hands
At the fire.

If there is a lake, notice the lake and not the hawk circling.
The stillness of the water Is the image for contemplation.

If there is a kiss, if there is a song of humility,
If there is a caress, a letter or crate of oranges,
Define the focus not the lips or touch
Or the sweet taste of the juice.

If the forsythia in bloom is placed at the center
The yellow is yellow, but speak about the yard
And the yard's health, and the forsythia
Will fade and drop its flowers
And the green leaves will take over
And the Plant will be transformed
Into an ordinary smudge In the garden.

Focus. Define me. Underline me.
Do not deflect me to the edge of the lake.
Do not push me to the side of the sea.
Know that I am not just a row of daffodils
In the spring garden.

BOTTICELLI'S BIRTH OF VENUS

***She came in such still water, and so nursed In silence,
beauty blessed and beauty cursed.***
—Hart Crane

I am standing on dry land, the earth of Vermont,
The soil in Texas, the land spread out in
Red clay and fields of open spring.
I stand having emerged from the sea
Or from dream songs the sparrows imitate.

I was conceived from the father,
Emerged from ground whale bones
And the tumult of the sea floor, but
I am more than a siren, more than a myth.
I arrived between conflicting forces:
On one side god of the wind disguised as fate,
And on the other the goddess of spring
Standing on the shore with a pink cloak
Embroidered with myrtle.

Do not look upon me as carved ivory.
Do not think of me as weaned from sea milk.
Do not try to cover me with your modesty.

I am not innocent born, not the creation
Of honeycombs, heaven's wish, or sea gardens.
I am fluid as flesh to a sculptor's eye.
Press your fingers against my body
And you will feel not stone, not myth
But the warmth of mortal flesh..

See how I step off the gilded shell?
See the showers of the first-born roses?
This is the beginning; roses will wither but thorns endure.
The shell will be worn to nothing under the tide,
But the tide will endure.
Do not confuse me with the star of the sea.
I am born of agony.

WOMEN OPPRESSED

"...to be loved and found magical, like a secret..."
—Anne Sexton

I was born in the shadow of castles.
I am a common woman
With hooves at the tips of my legs.

I drink the water from the stream beside me.
I wear flowers in my hair.
I lean my back against the rocks.
I know of no other tenderness.

I am the mother of goat men
Sucking milk from my breasts.
I seek the pleasure of this draining
For there is no other way to express
What is gathered in the reservoir of my body.

I am a woman ignored.

AFTER THE ORGASM

I, being born a woman and distressed
By all the needs and notions of my kind,
Am urged by your propinquity to find
Your person fair, and feel a certain zest
To bear your body's weight upon my breast:
—Edna St. Vincent Millay

Do not touch the flame of my body
After our lovemaking.
No cold lips, no tender words.
I am through with the release.
My nerves and muscles
Have done their work.

Let my nipples simmer.
Let the rim of my breasts
Cool back to skin and less heat.

Do not caress me
As if your can reshape me
Back into a woman.
I want to linger for awhile
And remember the feel
Of your fire on my tongue.
I want to move like burning silk,
Writhe in the memory
Of being ignited.

Let me recover
In my slow breathing.

Let me settle in silence
Like ash.

CONCLUSION

I have made my choice, after all

WHEN I AM OLD

But one man loved the pilgrim soul in you,
—William Butler Yeats

When I open this book of poems on my lap,
And the last breath of winter is at my lips,
I will still taste my words, notice they are warm,
Knowing the words could easily transform into tea.
As I turn the pages I still inhale
The aroma from words like Tennessee and Florida.

A poem is not a woman's breasts or her voice
Inside a poet's voice. A true poem
Is a slant of light on my face from the open window
As I still feel the sentences unbutton my dress once more.

When I am old and resting by the fire,
And the flames illuminate this book,
When the honey heat glazes me in sudden passion,
And you hear my voice, you will know I am
Reading poetry, a private whisper as I adjust my shawl.
I have made my choice, after all.

Author Profile

Christopher de Vinck, a husband, father, and grandfather, earned his doctoral degree from Columbia University and devoted 40 years to his career in public education. This is his 19th book. His previous books have been published by HarperCollins, Viking, Doubleday, Crossroad Books, Simon and Schuster (Four Winds Press), Hodder, Paulist Press, Paraclete Press, Loyola Press, and the Upper Room. Over 300 of Christopher's op/ed essays have been published in *The New York Times*, *The Wall Street Journal*, *The Chicago Tribune*, *USA Today*, *The Pittsburgh Post-Gazette*, *The NJ Record*, *The Dallas Morning News*, *The National Catholic Reporter*, *Readers Digest*, *Good Housekeeping*. *He is* a contributing columnist for *The Dallas Morning News*.